GREETINGS FROM SOMEWHERE

The Mystery of the Suspicious Spices

BY HARPER PARIS • ILLUSTRATED BY MARCOS CALO

LITTLE SIMON

New York   London   Toronto   Sydney   New Delhi

LITTLE SIMON

An imprint of Simon & Schuster Children's Publishing Division • 1230 Avenue of the Americas, New York, New York 10020 • First Little Simon hardcover edition December 2014 • Copyright © 2014 by Simon & Schuster, Inc. All rights reserved, including the right of reproduction in whole or in part in any form. LITTLE SIMON is a registered trademark of Simon & Schuster, Inc., and associated colophon is a trademark of Simon & Schuster, Inc. For information about special discounts for bulk purchases, please contact Simon & Schuster Special Sales at 1-866-506-1949 or business@simonandschuster.com. The Simon & Schuster Speakers Bureau can bring authors to your live event. For more information or to book an event contact the Simon & Schuster Speakers Bureau at 1-866-248-3049 or visit our website at www.simonspeakers.com. Designed by John Daly. The text of this book is set in ITC Stone Informal. Manufactured in the United States of America 1114 FFG

10 9 8 7 6 5 4 3 2 1

Library of Congress Cataloging-in-Publication Data

Paris, Harper. The mystery of the suspicious spices / by Harper Paris ; illustrated by Marcos Calo. — First edition. pages cm. — (Greetings from somewhere ; #6) Summary: In a Mumbai market, twin detectives Ethan and Ella investigate why a spice seller's spices have suddenly gone bad. [1. Mumbai (India)—Fiction. 2. India—Fiction. 3. Spices—Fiction. 4. Brothers and sisters—Fiction. 5. Twins—Fiction. 6. Mystery and detective stories.] I. Calo, Marcos, illustrator. II. Title. PZ7.P21748Mze 2014 [Fic]—dc23 2014000351

ISBN 978-1-4814-1468-5 (hc)

ISBN 978-1-4814-1467-8 (pbk)

ISBN 978-1-4814-1469-2 (eBook)

TABLE OF CONTENTS

CHAPTER 1

A New Mystery?

"This is the coolest castle I've ever seen!" Ethan Briar exclaimed.

"It's not a castle. It's a *palace*," his twin sister, Ella, corrected him. "It says so right here in Dad's guidebook. 'Taj Mahal' means 'crown of palaces.'"

Ethan shrugged. "Castle, palace, whatever. It's still awesome!"

"An emperor named Shah Jahan

built it in memory of his wife back in the sixteen hundreds," their dad, Andy, explained.

"It has become one of the most popular tourist attractions in the world," their mom, Josephine, added. "Millions of people visit it every year."

"Wow!" Ella stared in awe at the white marble building. It was really beautiful—and really big, too!

The Taj Mahal was the latest stop on the Briar family's trip across India. So far, they'd visited a tea plantation, a desert, and a snow-capped mountain. They had ridden on a small, old-fashioned train called a "toy train" that chugged up steep

hills. They'd seen lots of temples, including one shaped like a giant stone frog. Tomorrow morning, they were flying to the city of Mumbai, which was on the Arabian Sea. '

Mrs. Briar was a travel writer for their hometown newspaper, the *Brookeston Times*. Her job was to write articles about interesting places all over the world. The Briars had already been to Venice, Italy; Paris, France; and Beijing, China. Their last adventure before India was a safari in Africa! While Mrs. Briar worked,

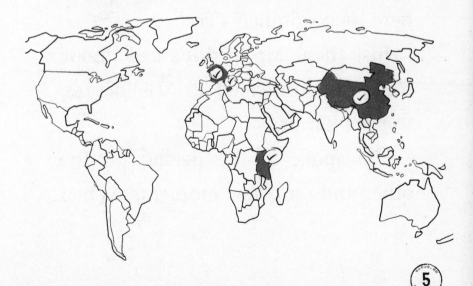

Mr. Briar homeschooled Ethan and Ella in their second-grade lessons.

Mr. Briar pointed his camera at the twins. "Let me get a photo of you kids standing on the steps. Wait. Why can't I see anything?"

"You forgot to take off the lens cap, Dad," Ethan told him.

Mr. Briar laughed. "Oh, right! Okay, here we go. Smile!" *Click!*

Just then, Mrs. Briar's cell phone rang. She answered it. "Hello? Yes, this is Jo Briar."

She spoke to the person on the other end for a few moments. When

she hung up, she said, "That was Mr. Deepak Singh. He's an old friend of Grandpa Harry, and he lives in Mumbai. He invited us to dinner tomorrow night."

"Is he an archaeologist like Grandpa Harry?" Ethan asked.

"No. He's a spice merchant," Mrs. Briar replied.

Ella looked thoughtful. "You mean he sells spices? Like the ones in the grocery store?"

Mrs. Briar smiled. "Sort of. In India, spices are very special. They are incredibly pure and delicious."

"Deepak is going to call me back later with his address and directions,"

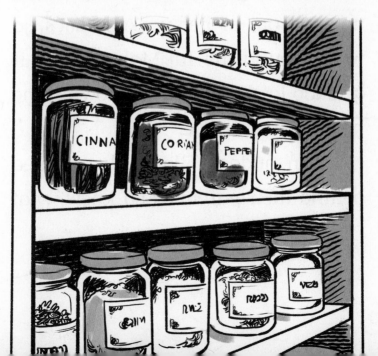

Mrs. Briar went on. "He had to get off the phone rather suddenly. Apparently, there was some trouble at his spice store."

"What kind of trouble?" Ella asked curiously.

"I'm not sure. Maybe we'll find out tomorrow night." Mrs. Briar pulled a notepad out of her pocket. "Let's go walk around the Taj Mahal before it gets too late! I want to jot down some notes for my article."

Ethan nudged Ella as they trailed behind their parents. Ella knew what her brother was thinking. Sometimes "trouble" meant "mystery." And the twins *loved* mysteries!

CHAPTER 2

The City of Seven Islands

The following afternoon, the Briars checked into their hotel in Mumbai. They were tired after their journey but excited to be in the big city.

Ella set her suitcase on the floor of her and Ethan's room and glanced out the window. There was a lush green garden with a row of feathery palm trees. Just beyond were the gentle blue waters of the Arabian Sea. She could make out a row of skyscrapers in the distance.

Ethan plopped down on one of the beds and opened up their dad's laptop. After a moment he announced: "We got an e-mail from Grandpa Harry!"

Ella sat down next to him. The twins always looked forward to Grandpa Harry's e-mails. He lived near Brookeston, and they hadn't seen him in months.

To: ethanella@eemail.com
From: gpaharry@eemail.com
Subject: Welcome to Mumbai!

Hello, my dears. Mumba'ī mēṁ āpakā svāgata hai! (That means "Welcome to Mumbai" in Hindi!)

Mumbai is made up of seven islands, including one called Old Woman Island. There are islands outside of Mumbai, too, like Elephanta Island. When I went there I explored its ancient caves and dug up some very old coins.

My friend Deepak owns a spice store in the Kamala Market in Mumbai. His father used to own it. I hope you get a chance to visit the store.

Love,
Grandpa Harry
PS Deepak has a younger brother named Tufan. I'm not sure if he still lives in Mumbai.

Ethan reached into his pocket
and pulled out his lucky gold coin.
Grandpa Harry
had given it
to him just
before the
Briars left
Brookeston.
It had a
hawk on one
side and a globe
on the other.

"I wonder if Grandpa Harry found
my coin on Elephanta Island," Ethan
murmured.

"Maybe!" Ella got out her purple notebook and opened it to a blank page. The notebook had been *her* going-away present from Grandpa Harry.

Ethan smiled to himself. His sister was always writing down notes about everything.

Ella found a pen and wrote:

Visit Deepak's spice store.
Deepak has a brother named Tufan.

Ella closed her notebook and gazed out the window. In the beginning, she and Ethan had not been too happy about going on a trip around the world. They hadn't wanted to leave Grandpa Harry or their friends—especially their best friends Hannah and Theo.

The twins still missed everyone. But their trip had been pretty great so far. In fact, they'd had amazing adventures in every place they'd visited.

Ella wondered what brand-*new* adventures awaited them in Mumbai!

CHAPTER 3

Deepak and Sani

"Are we there yet?" Ethan asked. "I'm starving!"

"Almost," Mr. Briar replied as he squinted at a map. "I think we turn right at that movie theater."

"Actually, I think we turn left at that café," Mrs. Briar said, pointing.

The Briars were walking through downtown Mumbai. They were on

their way to have dinner with Deepak
and his wife, Sani.

The twins liked the bustling city.
Double-decker buses rumbled along-
side motorcycles and bicycles. Neon
signs in English and Hindi blinked

against the twilight sky.

"Look out for the cow!" Ella cried out suddenly.

The Briars stepped aside as a brown and white cow walked past them on the narrow street. Behind the cow, several cars honked their horns.

The cow wasn't the first animal the Briars had seen in Mumbai. Earlier, they'd spotted goats weaving through traffic. They had even seen a monkey jumping around on the sidewalk!

There was a long line of people waiting to buy tickets at the movie theater. "We should see a Bollywood film while we're here," Mr. Briar remarked.

"You mean a *Hollywood* film?" Ethan asked, confused.

"No, *Bollywood*. The word is a combination of 'Bombay,' which is the old name for Mumbai, and 'Hollywood.' Mumbai is like the Hollywood of India. They make lots of films here," Mr. Briar explained.

They soon reached the Singhs' apartment building. They rode the elevator up to the top floor, found the apartment, and rang the bell.

The door opened. A woman beamed at them. She had shiny black hair that was swept back in a ponytail.

"Welcome!" she said. "I am Sani. You must be the Briars."

Mrs. Briar introduced everyone. "I love your sari," she told Sani.

Ella looked at the red and yellow silk cloths that were draped around Sani's body. She had noticed that a lot of Indian women wore them.

"Thank you, Jo!" Sani said. "I must take you sari shopping while you are

in Mumbai. A blue one would look lovely with your blond hair. Now, please do come in! Deepak, our guests are here!" she called out over her shoulder.

There was a wonderful smell in

the air as the Briars walked into the apartment. Ethan couldn't figure out what it was, exactly. It smelled like a mixture of tomato soup, buttery pop-corn, and Grandpa Harry's herb garden back home.

A tall, slender man strolled into the living room. He wore a white tunic  that almost went to his knees and baggy pants. "Hello! Hello! I am Deepak. Please, come and sit. Dinner is ready. I hope you like vegetables."

Vegetables? Ethan made a face. He wasn't exactly a fan of them.

Everyone sat down at the table. Ethan

dug into his food. To his surprise, it was delicious!

"What are we eating? It's fantastic!" Mr. Briar told Deepak and Sani.

"We're having lentils with spiced vegetables and basmati rice," Sani explained. "The yogurt with almonds and spices is called *shrikhand*. The flatbread is called *chapati*. We're also having mango chutney, which is like relish, and *koshimbir*, which is a cucumber and carrot salad with mint." She added, "The spices are from Deepak's store."

"My father told me that you have the best spice store in all of

Mumbai," Mrs. Briar said.

Deepak frowned and looked away. Sani touched his arm.

Mrs. Briar looked startled. "I'm sorry. Did I say something wrong?"

"My store is no longer the best spice store in Mumbai. In fact, it is far from it," Deepak said with a sigh.

CHAPTER 4
An Unhappy Surprise

"What do you mean?" Mrs. Briar asked Deepak, concerned.

"Yesterday, when you and I were talking on the phone, Mrs. Gupta came by the store," Deepak explained. "She is one of my oldest and most loyal customers. She had bought some saffron from me for an important dinner she was preparing."

"And?" Mr. Briar asked.

Deepak's face turned red. "She said that my saffron was terrible and that it ruined the meal!"

"She said she would never shop at Deepak's store again," Sani added.

"Oh no. That's awful!" Mrs. Briar exclaimed.

"Have any of your customers ever complained before?" Ella piped up.

Deepak shook his head. "Never. My spices are the highest quality. People come from far away to shop at my store."

"What *is* saffron, anyway?" Ethan asked. It sounded like the name of a planet—or a superhero.

"Saffron is a very valuable spice. It has a honey flavor. The spice is red, but it turns foods yellow," Deepak replied.

Ella pulled her purple notebook out of her bag. "What other spices do you sell?" she asked Deepak.

"I sell many, many spices," Deepak said. "In addition to saffron, I sell turmeric, tamarind, ginger, coriander. . . ."

Ella flipped to a blank page and began writing as Deepak described his spices.

Saffron:	Very valuable. Honey flavor. The spice is red, but it turns food yellow.
Turmeric:	Slightly bitter. Golden-orange color.
Tamarind:	Sweet and sour. Used in desserts.
Ginger:	Good in curries.
Coriander:	Tastes like oranges.
Cinnamon:	Dad always puts it in our hot chocolate. It's yummy!

Ella stopped writing and flipped to the previous page. It said: *Visit Deepak's spice store* and *Deepak has a brother named Tufan.*

Ella wondered if Tufan worked at the spice store too. She also wondered if there was a mystery here that needed to be solved. What had happened to Deepak's saffron to make it taste so bad?

Ella turned to her parents. "Can we visit Deepak's spice store?"

"Of course!" Mr. Briar replied.

Mrs. Briar nodded.

"Why don't you come tomorrow morning?" Deepak suggested. "Hopefully, there will be no more unpleasant surprises—or unhappy customers!"

CHAPTER 5
Trouble at the Market

It was already hot and muggy out when the Briars took a taxi to the Kamala Market. Ethan liked the taxi, which was not a car but an electric rickshaw. It looked like a combination of a golf cart and a motorcycle!

The Kamala Market was near the water. The twins had never been to a market like this before. It wasn't like a farmers' market or a flea market. It wasn't like a shopping mall, either.

Instead, it was a long, narrow alley crammed with tiny stores and stalls. Awnings stretched overhead and provided shade from the sun. Workers carried large boxes and burlap sacks on their heads. Delivery trucks came and went, revving their engines noisily.

The Briars got out of the taxi and started down the busy alley. It was so jam-packed that it was hard to move. Ella remembered when she and Ethan had gotten lost in the Forbidden City in Beijing. She reached for her mother's hand. She noticed that Ethan was holding their father's hand, too.

As the Briars made their way through the market, they saw many incredible things for sale. They saw glittering jewelry and saris in rainbow colors. They saw towers of pineapples, baskets of purple eggplants, and fruits and vegetables they couldn't even identify. They saw buckets of exotic flowers and garlands of blossoms hanging from wooden rafters.

Mrs. Briar stopped in front of a rack of gold silk slippers. "Aren't these lovely?" she gushed, snapping a picture.

Nearby, Mr. Briar tried on a big straw hat. "How do I look?" he asked with a chuckle.

The family finally arrived at Deepak's store. It was wedged between a clothing boutique and an electronics shop. The sign said: SINGH & SONS SPICE COMPANY.

Like all the other stores, Singh & Sons opened up to the alley. Out front, neat rows of spices in metal bowls were lined up on a table. Some spices were bright orange; others were golden yellow; and yet others were emerald green.

Deepak and Sani appeared in the entryway and waved to the Briars.

"Good morning! I am very glad you made it!" Deepak called out.

Deepak and Sani gave the Briars a tour of the store. Shelves were crammed with jars of spices. Bins on the floor held

even more spices. The air smelled like gingerbread cookies, autumn leaves, and dried flowers.

"By the way, I am happy to report that I have had no more complaints from my customers," Deepak told the Briars. "I suppose what happened with Mrs. Gupta must have been an unfortunate accident."

Mrs. Briar's phone beeped with a message. She glanced at it quickly. "My editor wants me to interview some of the other shop owners here," she announced. "Do you all mind if I slip away for an hour or so?"

"You go on ahead, Jo. I want to check out a stall of antique maps that we passed back there," Mr. Briar said. "Kids, do you want to come with me? The maps might come in handy for our history lessons."

Antique maps? History lessons? The twins exchanged a frown.

"Ella and Ethan are welcome to stay with us," Sani spoke up.

"Yes!" Ella said immediately.

"Can we? Can we?" Ethan asked their parents.

Mrs. Briar turned to the Singhs. "Are you sure they won't be in your way?"

"Of course not! They can help me weigh spices," Sani replied.

"Stay right here until we get back, okay?" Mrs. Briar told the twins. "Promise you won't go anywhere."

"We promise!" the twins said in unison.

Mr. and Mrs. Briar said good-bye and headed out into the market. Deepak greeted some customers. Sani led Ethan and Ella to the back of the store. She showed them the special scale for weighing spices.

Sani was scooping some cinnamon out of a glass jar when a man burst into the store.

"You are the worst spice merchant in all of India!" he yelled.

CHAPTER 6

On the Case

Sani and the twins rushed to the front of the store. The man now stood in the alley, his arms in the air.

"What is going on?" Sani cried out.

"I will tell you what is going on!" the bearded man burst out. "I bought some turmeric from this store yesterday. I was making my wife's favorite dish. But the turmeric was terrible!"

"B-but that's impossible!" Deepak sputtered.

A small crowd had gathered in the alley. Everyone was whispering.

"I was about to buy some ginger here. But perhaps I should buy it elsewhere," one woman said to another.

"I think that is a good idea. I know another spice store in this market," the other woman said.

The two women walked away. The bearded man left too, as did the rest of the crowd.

"This is a disaster!" Deepak moaned. "What happened with Mrs. Gupta was not a fluke, after all. Word of this will get around, and no one will come to Singh and Sons anymore. I am ruined!"

"Oh, Deepak!" Now Sani sounded worried, too.

The twins followed Deepak and Sani back into the store. Deepak sank into a chair and put his head in his hands. Sani made coffee on a tiny stove. Out in the alley, the hustle and bustle of the marketplace continued.

"I think you have a mystery on your hands," Ella told Deepak. "Ethan and I can help you. We're good at solving mysteries!"

Deepak glanced up with a puzzled

expression. "But you are just children!"

"When we were in Venice, we found a missing gondola," Ethan said.

"When we were in Paris, we found a stolen painting," Ella added. "We've solved mysteries in other places, too."

"Perhaps you *can* help me, then," Deepak admitted. "But . . . where do we start?"

Ella pulled her purple notebook out of her bag. "First, we need to ask you some questions. Like, what could have made your spices taste different? Do spices ever go bad?"

"Yes, eventually. But all my spices are

very new and fresh," Deepak replied.

Ella wrote down this information.

"Could animals have gotten into them? Or bugs?" Ethan piped up.

Deepak shook his head. "No. No animals. No bugs. I cover the spices carefully every night."

Sani handed Deepak a cup of coffee. She also passed around a plate of bread. "You detectives cannot solve a mystery on an empty stomach," she said, smiling at the twins. "I made these *paratha* this morning. They have cinnamon in them. I remember you said you like cinnamon."

"Thank you!" Ethan said, grabbing a piece of the bread.

He bit into it—and almost gagged.

The bread tasted awful!

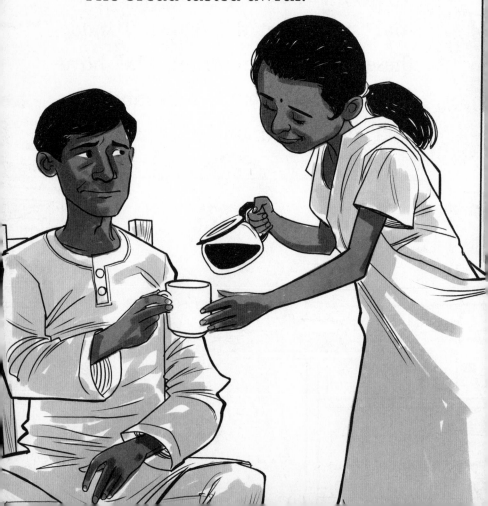

CHAPTER 7

Colorful Clues

Ella stared at Ethan, confused. Her brother's face was all scrunched up, as though he had swallowed a fly.

"Hey, what's wrong, Ethan?" she whispered.

"Uh . . . taste . . . the . . . bread," he whispered back.

Ella took a small bite. *Yuck!*

Sani was making more coffee at

the stove. "So how do you like the cinnamon *paratha*, children?" she called out cheerfully.

"It's great!" Ethan fibbed.

"Yum!" Ella added politely.

Deepak set down his coffee cup and frowned at the twins. "Are you sure? You both look a little pale."

Ella and Ethan squirmed. They didn't know what to do. Should they tell the truth? They didn't want to be rude.

Deepak picked up a piece of the *paratha* and took a bite.

"Sakala!" Deepak cried out. He spit out the bread and wiped his mouth with the back of his sleeve.

Sani whirled around. "Deepak! Why are you calling my *paratha* 'gross'?"

"Sani, this *paratha* is very, very salty. Did you accidentally use salt instead of cinnamon?" Deepak asked.

"What? No, of course not!" Sani replied.

She came over and tasted the bread. "*Sakala!* It *is* very salty. But how can that be?"

Deepak and Sani began speaking to each other in Hindi. While they were talking, Ethan inched closer to the stove.

He spotted the glass jar of cinnamon from before. He dipped a finger inside.

"*Ethan!* What are you doing?" Ella hissed.

"Just trust me," Ethan replied.

Ethan licked his finger to taste the cinnamon. He gasped.

"This isn't cinnamon. It's salt!" Ethan announced.

Deepak and Sani stopped talking. *"What?"* they exclaimed.

"Maybe you accidentally switched the labels on the cinnamon jar and the salt jar," Ethan said to Deepak.

"That is impossible! I am very careful. Besides, salt is white. Cinnamon is brown. The spice inside the jar labeled 'cinnamon' is brown," Deepak pointed out.

This gave Ella an idea. "Deepak, where is the spice that you sold to Mrs. Gupta? And where is the spice that you sold to the man with the beard?"

Deepak pointed to a couple of jars on the shelves. "The one on the left is the saffron. I sold some to Mrs. Gupta the day before yesterday. The one on the right is the turmeric. I sold some to the man with the beard yesterday."

Ella got the jars from the shelves. She then flipped through her notebook until she found the page about the spices.

Saffron: Very valuable. Honey flavor. The spice is red, but it turns foods yellow.

Turmeric: Slightly bitter. Golden-orange color.

Ella read over her notes. Then she compared them to the spices in the jars. The saffron was red, just like it was supposed to be. And the turmeric was golden-orange.

Ella scooped out samples of the two spices. She tasted each one. They were both really salty!

Then she noticed something else. The saffron and turmeric had left stains on her fingers. They looked almost like dye stains.

"I think I know what happened!" Ella announced.

CHAPTER 8

He's Getting Away!

Ella held up both her hands for the others to see. She fluttered her red- and orange-stained fingers.

"I think someone dyed salt with food coloring to make it look like saffron, turmeric, and cinnamon. Then they replaced the *real* spices with the dyed salt!" Ella explained.

"What?" Deepak burst out. Sani

looked shocked.

Ethan nodded, then started checking out the other spices. "This one is salty," he said, sampling from a jar labeled "coriander." "So is this one. But this isn't salty at all. And neither is this one."

The four of them went around tasting samples from the other jars.

Eventually, they figured out that half of the spices had been replaced by dyed salt. The other half were okay.

"Do you know anyone who would have replaced your spices with salt?" Ethan asked Deepak.

Deepak shook his head. "No. There is no one!"

Ella went through her notebook again and reread her entries. "Who else works at Singh and Sons? Grandpa Harry said you have a brother named Tufan. Does he work here too?"

"Tufan *used* to work here, when our father owned the store," Deepak replied. "When our father retired and left me in charge of the store, Tufan was upset. He quit and opened another spice store in this market."

Ethan raised his eyebrows at Ella. Ella frowned. They were both thinking the same thing. Could Tufan have tampered with Deepak's spices?

"I think we should go talk to your brother," Ethan said to Deepak.

Ethan and Ella followed Deepak through the Kamala Market. It was even busier than when they had first arrived. Fortunately, they didn't run into their parents. After all, they had

promised not to leave Singh & Sons.

As the twins trailed behind Deepak, they passed lots of interesting-looking stores and stalls. Ella noticed a used-book stand. A rack of soccer jerseys caught Ethan's eye. But there was no time to browse or shop. They had to find Tufan!

"There!" Deepak said suddenly.

He pointed to a small store at the end of the alley. The sign on it said: SPICE PALACE.

A huge line had formed out front. A man stood in the entryway. He smiled smugly as he handed out bags of spices and stuffed wads of money into his pockets. With his dark hair and big eyes, he looked like a younger version of Deepak.

"Tufan!" Deepak called out.

Tufan glanced up. His smile fell when he saw his brother.

"I am sorry, everyone. Spice Palace is closed for the rest of the day!" Tufan announced.

With that, he turned around and disappeared into the crowd.

"He's getting away!" Ethan shouted.

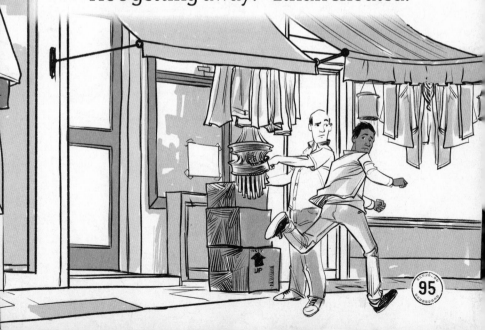

CHAPTER 9
The Two Detectives

Ethan stood on his tiptoes to see where Tufan had gone. He saw a flash of yellow near the rack of soccer jerseys.

Ethan took off running. He darted this way and that to avoid bumping into anyone.

Soon he was just a few feet behind Tufan. Thinking quickly, he yelled, "Look out for the cow!"

Tufan stopped in his tracks and peered around in confusion. It was just enough time for Ethan to catch up to him—and Deepak and Ella, too.

Deepak grabbed his brother's arm. "You cannot escape, Tufan. I know what you did!"

"What are you talking about, Deepak? I didn't do anything!" Tufan yelled.

"You replaced my spices with salt and tried to steal my customers," Deepak stated. "Of course, I never would have figured it out without these two young detectives!"

Ethan and Ella stood up very straight.

Tufan looked defeated. "This is our father's fault for leaving Singh and

Sons to you. It should have been *my* store!"

"I know you were unhappy with our father's decision, Tufan. But you should have talked to me. We could have worked this out. You should not have tried to destroy our family's store," Deepak told him.

"Yes, you are right," Tufan said, hanging his head. "I am sorry, Deepak. Will you ever forgive me?"

Deepak held out his hand. Tufan clasped it. The two brothers shook hands.

* * *

When Mr. and Mrs. Briar walked into Singh & Sons, the twins were helping Deepak and Sani throw out the dyed salts. Tufan had returned to his own store to retrieve all the spices that he had taken from Deepak's store.

Mrs. Briar apologized to the Singhs. "I'm sorry we were gone for so long. I managed to get lots of material for my article!"

"And I bought a couple of terrific antique maps," Mr. Briar said, patting his shopping bag. "So! What did we miss?"

"Well, let's see. We had some drama earlier. Someone had been meddling with my spices," Deepak replied.

"Really? How on earth did you figure that out?" Mrs. Briar asked, surprised.

Ethan caught Deepak's eye and held his finger to his lips. He didn't want their parents to know that they had left the store.

Deepak grinned and nodded. "I consulted some detective friends of mine," he said to Mr. and Mrs. Briar.

Mr. Briar whistled. "Wow! They sound like very good friends to have!"

"Indeed!" Deepak said merrily. He winked at Ethan and Ella. They winked back at him.

Sani held out several small packages. "These are for you," she told the twins.

Ethan and Ella opened their packages. Ethan's contained a jar of cinnamon that had been engraved with a bird. Ella's contained a jar of saffron that had been engraved with a flower.

"Thank you!" they said excitedly. They admired the engravings.

"You're welcome. But we are the ones who should be thanking *you*," Sani replied.

"For helping us around the store this morning," Deepak added quickly.

"Sounds like you kids have become quite the spice experts," Mr. Briar remarked.

"We sure have!" Ethan said, elbowing Ella.

The twins exchanged a secret smile.

GLOSSARY

Mumba'ī mēṁ āpakā
svāgata hai! = Welcome to Mumbai!

Sakala! = Gross

*All words are in Hindi.

GREETINGS FROM
SOMEWHERE

MACHU PICCHU, PERU

GREETINGS FROM
SOMEWHERE
The
Mystery Across
the Secret Bridge

MACHU PICCHU, PERU
7

BY HARPER PARIS • ILLUSTRATED BY MARCOS CALO

Ethan Briar peered over the edge of the rocky cliff. "Whoa! That's a big drop!" he exclaimed. The roaring river down below now looked like a skinny ribbon.

"I believe you," said his twin sister, Ella, nervously. She kept her gaze straight ahead and clutched Butterscotch's reins. "Butterscotch" was the nickname she had given her Peruvian Paso horse. Ethan called his horse "Keeper" because he liked soccer.

Ella, Ethan, and their parents, Andy and Josephine, were horseback riding through the Sacred Valley in

Peru. The guide, Fernando, led their tour group along a dirt path that went steeply uphill. Towering mountains, lush, green grass, and colorful flowers surrounded them.

The Sacred Valley was the Briars' second stop in Peru. Their first stop had been the capital city of Lima. In Lima, they explored catacombs— ancient passageways underground— and swam in the Pacific Ocean. It was the same ocean they swam in when they'd visited their family friends in California the year before!

The Briar family was taking a big

trip around the world. Mrs. Briar was writing about their trip for the *Brookeston Times*, which was their hometown newspaper. The family had already been to Italy, France, China, Kenya, and India since leaving Brookeston several months ago.

"Kids, check it out!" Mr. Briar said, pointing.

The twins gasped. Up ahead was a sight that was both totally awesome and totally confusing at the same time! Wide terraces had been carved into the side of a mountain. Along those terraces were little pools.

Hundreds of white patches covered the pools, like snow.

Except that it wasn't snow.

"We have arrived at the *salineras de Maras*, or the salt mines of Maras," Fernando, the guide, explained. "The people of this area have harvested salt here since before the time of the Incas. There is natural salt water inside this mountain. The people let the salt water collect into pools. They wait for the water to evaporate, or dry up, in the sun. What remains are those white patches of salt you see before you."

"Cool!" Ethan said. He and Ella knew about evaporation from their dad's science lessons. He was home-schooling the second graders.

"What are Incas?" Ella whispered to Mr. Briar.

"The Incas were a civilization of people who used to live here more than five hundred years ago," Mr. Briar whispered back.

"Can we walk around?" Mrs. Briar asked Fernando as she tucked her blond hair under her helmet.

"*Sí*. We will tether our horses and explore the mines on foot," Fernando replied. "We will even be able to taste some of the salt."

People from the tour group began tying their horses to posts.

As Ella tied up her horse, she noticed a little boy nearby. A blue toy snake was draped across his shoulders.

"Isn't this great, Slither?" the little boy said to his snake.

Standing next to him was a teen-aged girl. She didn't look very happy.

Ella wondered who they were. But before she could find out, it was time to begin the tour of the salt mines.

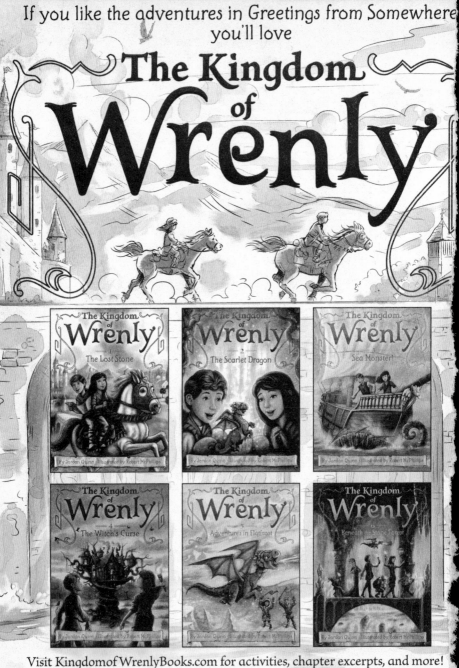